FIRST LOVE IN PARIS

First Love in Paris

Love Stories Around the World, Volume 1

Mikey

Published by Mikey, 2024.

This is a work of fiction. Similarities to real people, places, or events are entirely coincidental.

FIRST LOVE IN PARIS

First edition. April 26, 2024.

Copyright © 2024 Mikey.

ISBN: 979-8224059485

Written by Mikey.

Dedication

To every dreamer who has wandered the streets of Paris in search of love, to every heart that has dared to believe in the magic of first love, and to every soul who has found solace in the pages of a book—I dedicate "First Love in Paris."

May this story be a beacon of hope, a symphony of emotions, and a reminder that love, in all its forms, is the greatest adventure of all.

With love and gratitude,

Mikey Katodiya

MIKEY KATODIYA

Foreword

To the Readers,

It is with great pleasure that I introduce you to "First Love in Paris," a captivating tale of love, resilience, and the timeless beauty of heartfelt connections. Within these pages, you will embark on a journey alongside Sophie and Alex, two souls whose love story transcends boundaries and touches the depths of the human heart.

As the author of this book, Mikey Katodiya, invites you into the enchanting world of Sophie and Alex, you will witness their highs and lows, their joys and sorrows, and ultimately, their unwavering commitment to each other. Set against the backdrop of the picturesque city of Paris, their love story unfolds like a delicate dance, weaving through the streets of romance and the avenues of personal growth.

"First Love in Paris" is not just a story; it is an exploration of the complexities of love—the passion, the challenges, and the profound impact it has on our lives. Through Sophie and Alex's journey, you will discover the enduring power of love to heal, to inspire, and to transform.

As you turn the pages of this book, may you be captivated by the magic of Paris, by the depth of emotions portrayed, and by the universal truth that love knows no bounds. Join Sophie and Alex on their quest for love, and let their story resonate with your own experiences, reminding you of the beauty and resilience of the human heart.

With warmth and anticipation,
Mikey Katodiya

Preface

Dear Reader,

Welcome to the enchanting world of "First Love in Paris," a tale that will take you on a journey of love, passion, and discovery through the streets of the City of Lights. As the author of this book, Mikey Katodiya, I am thrilled to share with you the captivating story of Sophie and Alex.

Paris, with its timeless allure and romantic charm, serves as the perfect backdrop for Sophie and Alex's love story. In these pages, you will experience the magic of the Eiffel Tower at twilight, the whispers of love in quaint Parisian cafes, and the transformative power of a love that knows no bounds.

"First Love in Paris" is more than just a love story; it is a reflection of the human experience—the joys of falling in love, the challenges of overcoming obstacles, and the resilience of the human spirit. Through Sophie and Alex's journey, you will be reminded of the universal truths of love—its ability to heal, to inspire, and to shape our lives in profound ways.

As you delve into these pages, I invite you to immerse yourself in the sights, sounds, and emotions of Paris, to feel the heartbeat of the city and the beating of Sophie and Alex's hearts. May their story ignite a spark of hope, passion, and belief in the enduring power of love.

Thank you for joining me on this unforgettable journey. I hope "First Love in Paris" touches your heart and leaves you with a renewed sense of love's beauty and possibility.

Warm regards,

Mikey Katodiya

Acknowledgements

I would like to extend my heartfelt gratitude to everyone who has contributed to the creation of "First Love in Paris." This book has been a labor of love, and I am immensely grateful for the support, inspiration, and dedication of those who have been part of this journey.

To Sophie and Alex, the protagonists of this story, thank you for allowing me to tell your tale of love, resilience, and growth. Your characters have inspired me, and I hope readers will find solace and joy in your journey.

To my family, friends, and loved ones, thank you for your unwavering support and encouragement throughout the writing process. Your belief in me has been a source of strength and motivation.

To the readers, thank you for embarking on this adventure with me. I hope "First Love in Paris" brings you moments of joy, reflection, and connection with the universal themes of love and human experience.

Warm regards,
Mikey Katodiya

Prologue

In the heart of Paris, where cobblestone streets echo with whispers of romance and the Seine River weaves tales of love, there exists a story that transcends time—a story of two souls destined to find each other amidst the bustling city's magic. This is the tale of Sophie and Alex, whose journey of love and discovery unfolds against the backdrop of Parisian beauty and the complexities of the human heart.

Sophie, with her infectious laughter and passion for art, embodies the spirit of Paris—a city that celebrates love in all its forms. Alex, with his quiet strength and unwavering devotion, complements Sophie's free-spirited nature, creating a harmony that defies words.

Their paths cross in a moment of serendipity, under the twinkling lights of the Eiffel Tower, where dreams take flight and hearts find solace. From that moment on, their lives intertwine in a dance of longing, desire, and the timeless allure of first love.

As we embark on this journey with Sophie and Alex, let us immerse ourselves in the enchanting world of "First Love in Paris," where every corner holds a secret, every glance carries a story, and every heartbeat resonates with the promise of a love that knows no bounds.

Welcome to their world—a world where love blossoms like springtime in Paris, where every moment is a treasure, and where the echoes of their love's melody linger long after the final page is turned.

ONE

The Encounter

The bustling streets of New York City buzzed with life as Sophie hurried along, her mind preoccupied with thoughts of work and deadlines. She had always been a career-driven woman, fiercely independent and focused on her goals. Yet, amidst the chaos of the city, there was a subtle longing for something more, something she couldn't quite define.

It was on a particularly busy Monday morning that their paths first crossed. Sophie was rushing to catch the subway when she accidentally bumped into someone, sending her papers scattering across the pavement. Flustered, she bent down to gather her things, only to find a pair of warm brown eyes looking back at her with a hint of amusement.

"I'm so sorry," the stranger said, extending a hand to help her up. "I should've been watching where I was going."

Sophie couldn't help but notice his genuine smile and friendly demeanor. "No, it's my fault. I was in a hurry," she replied, grateful for his assistance.

As they collected her papers together, their fingers briefly touched, sending a jolt of electricity through Sophie. It was a fleeting moment, but it left an indelible impression on her.

"Thanks for helping me," she said, offering a shy smile.

"Anytime," he replied, his smile widening. "I'm Alex, by the way."

"Sophie," she introduced herself, feeling a strange sense of connection with this stranger she had just met.

They parted ways at the subway station, but Sophie couldn't shake off the feeling that their encounter was more than just a random coincidence. There was a spark, a tiny ember of possibility that ignited something within her.

Over the next few days, Sophie found herself thinking about Alex more often than she cared to admit. She caught herself stealing glances at her phone, hoping for a message or a call that never came. It was both thrilling and frustrating, this newfound attraction to someone she barely knew.

One evening, as she was leaving the office, Sophie spotted Alex across the street, walking with a group of friends. Their eyes met briefly, and Sophie felt her heart skip a beat. She wanted to approach him, to strike up a conversation, but fear held her back. What if he didn't remember her? What if their initial encounter meant nothing to him?

As weeks passed, Sophie's thoughts kept drifting back to Alex. She found herself yearning for another chance meeting, a moment where they could talk and get to know each other better. She wondered if he felt the same way, if their brief connection had left a mark on him as it had on her.

Then, one day, fate intervened in the most unexpected way. Sophie received an invitation to a charity gala, organized by her company. It was a prestigious event, attended by influential figures from various industries. As she scanned the guest list, one name stood out among the RSVPs—Alex.

Heart racing with anticipation, Sophie decided to attend the gala, hoping that she would have the opportunity to see Alex again. She spent hours preparing for the event, choosing the perfect dress and rehearsing small talk in front of the mirror.

When the night of the gala arrived, Sophie arrived at the venue feeling a mix of excitement and nervousness. The ballroom was adorned with elegant decorations, and the air was filled with laughter and music. Sophie mingled with colleagues and clients, all the while keeping an eye out for Alex.

Then, she saw him—dressed in a sharp suit, his smile just as captivating as she remembered. Their eyes met across the room, and Sophie felt a surge of courage. She made her way through the crowd, determined to finally have a proper conversation with him.

"Alex," she said, approaching him with a smile.

"Sophie, it's great to see you again," Alex replied, his eyes lighting up with genuine pleasure.

They fell into easy conversation, exchanging stories and laughter as the night progressed. Sophie discovered that Alex was an entrepreneur with a passion for travel and adventure. He was charming, witty, and everything she had hoped for.

As the gala drew to a close, Alex asked Sophie if she would like to grab a coffee sometime. She agreed without hesitation, her heart soaring with excitement at the prospect of getting to know him better.

And so, their love story began—a chance encounter that blossomed into something beautiful and unexpected. Sophie realized that sometimes, the most meaningful connections come when you least expect them, in the midst of a busy cityscape where hearts collide and destinies intertwine.

TWO

Serendipitous Meetings

The coffee shop buzzed with activity as Sophie waited nervously for her meeting with Alex. It had been a week since the charity gala, and she couldn't shake off the excitement of getting to know him better. As she sipped her latte, memories of their first encounter replayed in her mind—the accidental bump on the busy New York street, the warmth of Alex's smile, and the spark of connection that had ignited between them.

When Alex arrived, their conversation flowed effortlessly, as if they had known each other for years. They talked about their passions, dreams, and shared love for exploring new places. Sophie was captivated by Alex's adventurous spirit and genuine curiosity about the world.

Over the next few weeks, Sophie and Alex met regularly, discovering common interests and deepening their connection. They explored different neighborhoods in the city, tried new restaurants, and even took a spontaneous road trip to a nearby beach town. Each moment spent together felt like a chapter in their evolving love story, a tapestry woven with laughter, shared secrets, and growing affection.

As their relationship blossomed, Sophie found herself opening up to Alex in ways she hadn't with anyone else. She shared her hopes, fears, and aspirations, knowing that he listened with genuine interest and understanding. Alex, in turn, revealed his vulnerabilities and past experiences, forging a bond built on trust and mutual respect.

Their serendipitous meetings continued to shape their love story, each encounter deepening their emotional connection. They navigated life's ups and downs together, offering support and encouragement during challenging times. Sophie found solace in Alex's presence, knowing that he was not just a romantic partner but also a confidant and a source of strength.

One evening, as they watched the sunset from a rooftop terrace, Alex turned to Sophie with a tender expression. "You know, I never expected to meet someone like you," he said, his voice filled with sincerity. "You've brought so much joy and meaning into my life."

Sophie smiled, her heart overflowing with love. "You've done the same for me," she replied, reaching for his hand.

Their relationship continued to evolve, marked by moments of laughter, shared dreams, and quiet understanding. They supported each other's goals and aspirations, celebrating milestones and facing challenges together as a team. Sophie felt grateful for the serendipitous twist of fate that had brought Alex into her life, turning a chance encounter into a deep and meaningful connection.

As time passed, Sophie and Alex's love story became a testament to the beauty of unexpected meetings and the power of genuine connection. They learned from each other, grew together, and cherished every moment of their journey.

One day, as they walked hand in hand through Central Park, Alex stopped beneath a blossoming cherry tree. He turned to Sophie, his eyes filled with love and devotion.

"Sophie," he began, his voice steady with emotion. "I've known since the day we met that you were someone special. Will you do me the honor of spending the rest of your life with me?"

Tears of joy welled up in Sophie's eyes as she nodded, her heart overflowing with love and gratitude. In that moment, surrounded by the beauty of nature and the warmth of Alex's love, she knew that their serendipitous meetings had led them to a lifetime of happiness together.

Their love story continued to unfold, with each chapter filled with laughter, love, and the magic of serendipity—the perfect blend of chance and destiny that had brought two hearts together in a love that was destined to last a lifetime.

THREE
Whispers of Love

As Sophie and Alex's relationship deepened, whispers of love filled the air, weaving a tapestry of emotions that bound them together. Their days were filled with stolen moments of affection, shared dreams, and the quiet reassurance of a love that grew stronger with each passing day.

One afternoon, as they wandered through a sun-kissed park, Alex stopped beneath a blossoming tree and turned to Sophie with a gentle smile. "Do you remember the first time we met?" he asked, his eyes sparkling with nostalgia.

Sophie nodded, a fond smile tugging at her lips. "How could I forget? It feels like a lifetime ago, yet the memory is as vivid as ever."

They reminisced about their serendipitous encounter on the bustling streets of New York, the accidental bump that sparked a connection neither of them could deny. Sophie marveled at how their paths had crossed at just the right moment, leading them to this beautiful chapter in their love story.

As they sat beneath the tree, Sophie felt a surge of gratitude for the love they shared. It was a love built on trust, respect, and a deep understanding of each other's hopes and dreams. They talked about their future together, envisioning a life filled with adventure, laughter, and unwavering support.

Days turned into weeks, and weeks turned into months, but their love only grew stronger with time. They celebrated milestones together, marking each moment with laughter and joy. Sophie found herself falling more deeply in love with Alex, cherishing every whispered "I love you" and tender gesture that spoke volumes without words.

One evening, as they watched the city lights twinkle from their balcony, Alex turned to Sophie with a glint of excitement in his eyes. "I have something to show you," he said, reaching into his pocket.

Curious, Sophie watched as Alex pulled out a small velvet box. Her heart fluttered with anticipation as he opened the box to reveal a sparkling ring—a symbol of his love and commitment.

"Sophie," Alex began, his voice filled with emotion. "You've brought so much happiness into my life, and I can't imagine a future without you by my side. Will you marry me?"

Tears of joy filled Sophie's eyes as she nodded, speechless with happiness. In that moment, surrounded by the glow of the city and the warmth of Alex's love, she knew that their love story had reached a new chapter—one filled with promises of forever and the sweet whispers of love that bound their hearts together.

Their engagement marked a new beginning, filled with wedding plans, shared dreams of a future together, and the unwavering certainty that they were meant to be. Sophie and Alex's love continued to blossom, a testament to the power of serendipity and the magic of whispered promises that echoed through the chapters of their love story.

FOUR
Navigating Challenges

As Sophie and Alex embarked on their journey towards marriage, they encountered challenges that tested their bond and strengthened their commitment to each other. Life's uncertainties and unexpected twists became chapters in their love story, shaping their relationship in profound ways.

One of the challenges they faced was balancing their busy careers with their growing relationship. Sophie's demanding job in marketing often required late nights and weekend meetings, while Alex's entrepreneurial ventures demanded flexibility and dedication. Despite the hectic schedules, they prioritized quality time together, carving out moments of togetherness amidst the chaos of their professional lives.

Communication became their lifeline, as they learned to express their needs, fears, and aspirations openly. They navigated conflicts with patience and understanding, resolving differences through heartfelt conversations and mutual respect. Their ability to communicate effectively strengthened their bond, transforming challenges into opportunities for growth and connection.

Another challenge arose when Sophie's family expressed concerns about their relationship. They questioned whether Alex was the right match for her, citing differences in background and career paths. Sophie faced internal struggles as she grappled with the expectations of her family and her own feelings for Alex.

Through it all, Alex remained steadfast in his love and support for Sophie. He reassured her of his commitment, standing by her side as they addressed concerns and bridged the gap between their worlds. Sophie found comfort in Alex's unwavering belief in their love, knowing that they were stronger together, despite external pressures.

Amidst the challenges, moments of joy and celebration punctuated their journey. They celebrated anniversaries, milestones, and shared accomplishments, finding solace in each other's victories and shared dreams. Their love became a source of strength, a beacon of hope that guided them through life's ups and downs.

One memorable evening, as they strolled hand in hand through a moonlit park, Alex pulled Sophie into his arms and whispered, "No matter what challenges come our way, I promise to always stand by you, to love you unconditionally, and to cherish every moment we share."

Sophie felt tears of gratitude and love fill her eyes as she hugged Alex tightly, knowing that their love was resilient, unwavering, and destined to overcome any obstacle. In that moment, surrounded by the beauty of nature and the warmth of Alex's embrace, she knew that their love story was not just about fairy-tale moments but also about navigating challenges together and emerging stronger as a couple.

Their journey continued, filled with twists and turns, joys and sorrows, but through it all, Sophie and Alex's love remained a constant—a testament to the power of resilience, commitment, and unwavering devotion that defined their love story.

FIVE

Embracing Growth

As Sophie and Alex's love story unfolded, they embraced moments of growth and transformation, learning valuable lessons that deepened their connection and enriched their relationship.

One of the significant milestones they experienced was moving in together. After months of shared experiences, laughter, and challenges, they decided it was time to take the next step in their commitment to each other. The process of merging their lives and belongings was both exciting and daunting, but they approached it with optimism and a shared vision for their future.

Their new home became a sanctuary—a place filled with love, laughter, and shared dreams. They decorated it together, infusing each room with their personalities and creating a space that reflected their journey as a couple. From cozy movie nights on the couch to spontaneous dance parties in the kitchen, every moment spent together in their home deepened their bond and brought them closer.

As they settled into their new routine, Sophie and Alex continued to support each other's personal growth and aspirations. Sophie pursued a passion project she had long dreamed of, while Alex delved into new entrepreneurial ventures with enthusiasm and determination. They celebrated each other's achievements, providing encouragement and unwavering support along the way.

Their relationship evolved into a partnership built on trust, mutual respect, and a shared sense of purpose. They navigated life's challenges together, finding strength in each other's presence and unwavering commitment. Through moments of joy and moments of hardship, their love remained a constant—a source of comfort, inspiration, and unwavering devotion.

One evening, as they sat on their balcony watching the sunset, Sophie turned to Alex with a smile. "Do you ever look back on our journey and marvel at how far we've come?" she asked, her eyes sparkling with love.

Alex nodded, his gaze filled with affection. "Every day, I'm grateful for the love we share and the growth we've experienced together," he replied, reaching for Sophie's hand.

Their love story was a testament to the beauty of growth, transformation, and the power of love to nurture and inspire. They embraced each new chapter with open hearts, knowing that their love would continue to flourish and evolve, guided by the strength of their connection and the depth of their feelings for each other.

As they looked towards the future, Sophie and Alex knew that their journey was far from over—it was just beginning, filled with endless possibilities, shared dreams, and a love that would stand the test of time. Their love story was a beautiful tapestry woven with moments of growth, laughter, joy, and unwavering devotion—a testament to the power of love to transform and inspire.

SIX
Dreams Fulfilled

As Sophie and Alex's love story continued to unfold, they found themselves on the brink of fulfilling their shared dreams and aspirations. Their journey together had been a testament to resilience, commitment, and unwavering devotion—a journey that led them to moments of joy, fulfillment, and the realization of their deepest desires.

One of their dreams was to travel the world together, exploring new cultures, experiencing different cuisines, and creating unforgettable memories. They had always been passionate about adventure and discovery, and now, with their love as their compass, they set out to turn their dream into reality.

Their first destination was Paris—a city of romance, art, and timeless beauty. Sophie and Alex wandered through cobblestone streets, marveled at iconic landmarks, and savored decadent pastries at quaint cafes. The magic of Paris enveloped them, igniting their passion for exploration and deepening their love for each other.

As they stood atop the Eiffel Tower, gazing at the city spread out before them, Sophie turned to Alex with a radiant smile. "This is everything I've ever dreamed of," she whispered, her heart overflowing with gratitude.

Alex wrapped his arms around her, pulling her close. "And we're just getting started," he replied, his eyes shining with excitement.

Their journey took them to exotic destinations, from the bustling streets of Tokyo to the serene beaches of Bali. They immersed themselves in new cultures, tried exotic foods, and shared moments of wonder and awe as they explored the world together. Each experience deepened their bond, creating a tapestry of memories that would last a lifetime.

One evening, as they watched the sunset from a secluded beach, Sophie leaned against Alex, her heart full of love. "Do you ever pinch yourself to make sure this is real?" she asked, her voice filled with wonder.

Alex chuckled, pressing a kiss to her forehead. "Every day," he replied, his gaze never leaving hers. "But I know that this—our love, our adventures, our dreams fulfilled—it's all real because we've built it together."

Their journey had been filled with ups and downs, twists and turns, but through it all, their love had remained steadfast—a beacon of hope, inspiration, and unwavering devotion. They had navigated challenges, embraced growth, and celebrated moments of joy and fulfillment, knowing that their love was the foundation upon which their dreams were built.

As they returned home, their hearts brimming with memories and their minds filled with dreams yet to be realized, Sophie and Alex knew that their love story was far from over. It was a story of endless possibilities, shared dreams, and a love that would continue to evolve and flourish, guided by the strength of their connection and the depth of their feelings for each other.

Their love story was a beautiful tapestry woven with threads of passion, adventure, and the magic of dreams fulfilled—a testament to the power of love to transform lives and inspire hearts to reach for the stars. And as they looked towards the future, hand in hand, Sophie and Alex knew that their greatest adventures were yet to come.

SEVEN
Everlasting Love

As Sophie and Alex's journey together continued, they found themselves entering a new chapter—one filled with the promise of everlasting love, shared dreams realized, and a future brimming with possibilities.

Their relationship had weathered storms and celebrated triumphs, but through it all, their love had remained unwavering—a beacon of hope, strength, and unwavering devotion.

One of the most significant moments in their journey came when they exchanged vows in a picturesque ceremony surrounded by loved ones. It was a day filled with joy, laughter, and tears of happiness as Sophie and Alex pledged their love and commitment to each other in front of family and friends.

As they stood hand in hand, gazing into each other's eyes, Sophie felt a profound sense of gratitude and love. "I promise to stand by you, to support you, and to love you unconditionally for all the days of my life," she whispered, her heart overflowing with emotion.

Alex smiled, his eyes shimmering with love. "I promise to cherish you, to protect you, and to be your partner in all things, now and forever," he vowed, his voice filled with sincerity.

Their wedding was a celebration of their love—a culmination of their journey together and a testament to the strength of their bond. They danced under the stars, surrounded by the warmth of their loved ones and the promise of a future filled with happiness and love.

As they settled into married life, Sophie and Alex continued to nurture their relationship, savoring each moment of togetherness and cherishing the memories they had created. They embarked on new adventures, pursued shared passions, and supported each other's dreams with unwavering dedication.

Years passed, and their love only grew deeper with time. They faced life's challenges together, drawing strength from their love and the unwavering support they provided each other. Through highs and lows, triumphs and trials, their love remained a constant—a source of comfort, joy, and inspiration.

One evening, as they sat on their balcony watching the sunset, Sophie leaned against Alex, her heart full of gratitude. "I never could have imagined a love as beautiful and enduring as ours," she whispered, her voice filled with emotion.

Alex wrapped his arms around her, pressing a kiss to her forehead. "Our love is the greatest adventure of all," he replied, his eyes shining with love. "And I wouldn't want to experience it with anyone but you."

Their love story had come full circle—a journey of growth, challenges, dreams realized, and a love that had stood the test of time. Sophie and Alex knew that their love was everlasting—a bond that would continue to thrive and inspire for years to come.

As they looked towards the future, hand in hand, Sophie and Alex knew that their love story was far from over—it was just beginning, filled with endless possibilities, shared dreams, and a love that would last a lifetime and beyond. And as they embraced each new day together, they did so with hearts full of gratitude, love, and the unwavering certainty that they were meant to be—forever and always.

EIGHT
Forever Begins

Sophie and Alex's love story had traversed through the ebbs and flows of life, shaping them into a couple filled with resilience, understanding, and enduring love. As they entered the eighth chapter of their journey, they stood at the threshold of a new beginning—a chapter where forever truly began.

Their marriage had been a testament to their commitment and devotion to each other. They had weathered storms together, celebrated triumphs, and built a life filled with love, laughter, and shared dreams. Now, as they looked towards the future, they knew that every moment was a precious gift to be cherished.

One of their dreams had always been to start a family—a dream that grew stronger with each passing day. Sophie and Alex talked about their hopes for the future, imagining a home filled with the laughter of children, the warmth of family gatherings, and the joy of watching their family grow.

Months turned into years, and their dream of starting a family became a reality. Sophie's laughter filled their home as they welcomed their first child—a beautiful baby girl named Emma. The moment Sophie held Emma in her arms, she knew that their love had created something truly magical—a bond that transcended words and filled their hearts with immeasurable joy.

As they navigated the challenges and joys of parenthood together, Sophie and Alex's love deepened even further. They marveled at the wonder of watching Emma grow, her laughter becoming the soundtrack of their lives and her milestones marking new chapters in their journey as a family.

Their love story continued to evolve, shaped by the everyday moments of love, laughter, and shared experiences. They celebrated anniversaries, milestones, and cherished family traditions that bound them together in love and unity.

One evening, as they sat by the fireplace, Emma nestled in between them, Sophie turned to Alex with a smile. "Our love has given us the greatest gift of all," she said, her eyes filled with love and gratitude.

Alex nodded, his gaze full of adoration for his family. "Every moment with you and Emma is a blessing," he replied, wrapping his arm around Sophie.

Their home was filled with love—a love that grew stronger with each passing day, a love that was the foundation of their family, and a love that would guide them through life's journey together.

Sophie and Alex knew that their love story was far from over—it was a story of a family united by love, laughter, and the promise of a future filled with endless possibilities. As they embraced each new day, they did so with hearts full of gratitude, love, and the unwavering certainty that their forever had truly begun.

NINE

A Legacy of Love

Sophie and Alex's journey together had encompassed a myriad of experiences—love, challenges, growth, and the joys of building a family. As they entered the final chapter of their story, they reflected on the legacy of love they had created—a legacy that would endure for generations to come.

Their family had grown over the years, with Emma now a bright young woman with dreams of her own. She had inherited her parents' sense of adventure, curiosity, and love for life, embodying the values that Sophie and Alex had instilled in her from a young age.

Together, as a family, they embarked on new adventures, explored new horizons, and created memories that would be treasured for a lifetime. From family vacations to meaningful traditions, every moment shared reinforced the bonds of love and unity that defined their family.

As Sophie and Alex watched Emma pursue her dreams with passion and determination, they knew that their love had laid the foundation for her success and happiness. They had taught her the value of love, kindness, resilience, and the importance of following one's heart.

One day, as they gathered for a family dinner, Emma turned to her parents with a smile. "Thank you for everything," she said, her voice filled with gratitude. "You've given me a life filled with love, support, and endless opportunities."

Sophie and Alex exchanged a glance, their hearts swelling with pride and love for their daughter. "You've always been our greatest joy," Sophie replied, reaching for Emma's hand.

Their home was filled with love—a love that transcended time and space, a love that had woven their family together in a tapestry of shared experiences, cherished moments, and unwavering devotion.

As Sophie and Alex looked back on their journey—the serendipitous meetings, the challenges overcome, the dreams realized, and the legacy of love they had created—they knew that their story was one of enduring love, resilience, and the power of family.

Their love story had come full circle, from chance encounters to building a life together, from navigating challenges to embracing growth, and from dreams fulfilled to creating a legacy of love that would live on in the hearts of their family for generations to come.

As they embraced each other, surrounded by the warmth of their family and the love that filled their home, Sophie and Alex knew that their love story would continue to inspire, uplift, and guide their family on the journey of life—a journey marked by love, laughter, and the everlasting bond of family. And as they looked towards the future, they did so with hearts full of gratitude, love, and the knowledge that their legacy of love would endure for eternity.

TEN

The Continuation of Love's Journey

Sophie and Alex sat together in the cozy warmth of their living room, reminiscing about their journey—the twists and turns, the highs and lows, and the unwavering love that had carried them through it all. As they entered this final chapter, they reflected on the continuation of their love's journey—a journey filled with memories, shared experiences, and the promise of a future woven with love's enduring thread.

Their home had become a sanctuary—a place where laughter echoed through the halls, where memories adorned every corner, and where love radiated from every heartbeat. It was a testament to the life they had built together, a life filled with love, joy, and the beauty of everyday moments.

As they looked back on their adventures—the trips taken, the dreams pursued, and the challenges overcome—they marveled at the depth of their bond. Their love had weathered storms and basked in sunshine, growing stronger with each passing day, each shared smile, and each whispered "I love you."

One evening, as they sat hand in hand on their balcony, watching the stars twinkle in the night sky, Sophie turned to Alex with a soft smile. "Do you remember when we first met?" she asked, her eyes twinkling with nostalgia.

Alex nodded, a fond smile playing on his lips. "How could I forget? It feels like a lifetime ago, yet it's as clear as day in my memory," he replied, his gaze filled with love.

Their love story had begun with a chance encounter, a serendipitous moment that had set their hearts on a path intertwined with destiny. From that moment onwards, they had navigated life's journey together, hand in hand, heart to heart.

As they embraced the present, Sophie and Alex looked towards the future with hope and excitement. They knew that their love's journey was far from over—it was a story that would continue to unfold, with new chapters waiting to be written, new adventures to embark upon, and new memories to create.

Their love had stood the test of time, a beacon of hope, strength, and unwavering devotion. It was a love that had shaped their lives, defined their family, and inspired all who crossed their path.

And as they sat together, basking in the glow of love's enduring flame, Sophie and Alex knew that their love's journey was a beautiful tapestry—a tapestry woven with threads of love, laughter, shared dreams, and the promise of a forever that would never fade.

Their love's journey was a story of love's timeless embrace, a story that would echo through the ages—a testament to the power of love to transform, to heal, and to illuminate the path forward.

As they whispered promises of forever to each other, under the starlit sky, Sophie and Alex knew that their love's journey would continue, guided by the light of their love and the promise of a future filled with endless possibilities. And with hearts full of gratitude and love, they embarked on the next chapter of their love's journey—a chapter that held the promise of a love that would last for eternity.

ELEVEN
The Journey Continues

Sophie and Alex's love story had traversed through the seasons of life, from the blossoming of young love to the strength of enduring companionship. As they embarked on the next chapter of their journey, they embraced the beauty of the present while eagerly anticipating the adventures that lay ahead.

Their family had grown with the addition of their second child, a charming son named Liam. His laughter added a new melody to their home, weaving joy and excitement into their everyday lives. Sophie and Alex marveled at the wonder of parenthood once again, cherishing each moment spent watching Liam grow and discover the world around him.

With Emma and Liam by their side, Sophie and Alex's family was complete—a testament to the love and commitment that had guided their journey. They reveled in family traditions, from cozy movie nights to holiday gatherings filled with laughter and love. Their home was a sanctuary, a place where memories were made and love thrived.

As Sophie and Alex looked towards the future, they embraced new opportunities and experiences. They traveled to new destinations, explored new hobbies, and continued to nurture their individual passions while supporting each other's dreams. Their love was a source of strength, a beacon of light that illuminated their path forward.

One evening, as they sat together on the porch swing, watching the sun set in a blaze of colors, Sophie leaned her head on Alex's shoulder. "Do you ever think about all we've been through?" she asked softly, her eyes reflecting the hues of the sky.

Alex smiled, wrapping his arm around her. "I do," he replied, his voice filled with warmth. "Every chapter of our story has led us to this moment, and I wouldn't change a thing."

Their journey had been a tapestry of love, woven with threads of laughter, tears, triumphs, and challenges. Each chapter had shaped them, strengthened their bond, and deepened their appreciation for the gift of love.

As they sat together, enveloped in the tranquility of the evening, Sophie and Alex knew that their journey would continue to unfold, filled with new beginnings, shared experiences, and the timeless beauty of love's embrace. And with hearts intertwined, they welcomed the next chapter of their love story with open arms, eager to see where the journey would take them next.

TWELVE
A Love That Endures

Sophie and Alex's love story had spanned the years, weaving a tapestry of shared experiences, cherished memories, and the enduring strength of their bond. As they entered the twelfth chapter of their journey, they marveled at the depth of their love—a love that had weathered storms, celebrated triumphs, and remained steadfast through the passage of time.

Their children, Emma and Liam, had grown into remarkable individuals, each with their own dreams and aspirations. Sophie and Alex supported them wholeheartedly, encouraging them to pursue their passions and embrace life's adventures with courage and determination.

As a family, they continued to create moments of joy and laughter, from family vacations to simple evenings spent playing games and sharing stories. Their home was filled with love—a love that echoed in the laughter of their children, the warmth of shared meals, and the comfort of being together.

Sophie and Alex's relationship had evolved into a partnership built on mutual respect, trust, and unwavering support. They faced life's challenges together, drawing strength from their love and the bond they had nurtured over the years.

One afternoon, as they sat in their garden, sipping tea and enjoying the tranquility of nature, Sophie turned to Alex with a smile. "Our love has endured through so much," she remarked, her eyes filled with gratitude.

Alex nodded, his gaze filled with love. "And it will continue to do so," he replied, reaching for her hand. "Our journey together is a testament to the power of love to overcome any obstacle."

Their love story was a legacy—a legacy of love, resilience, and the beauty of a life lived with purpose and passion. They looked towards the future with hope and excitement, knowing that their love would continue to guide them through life's joys and challenges.

As the sun set on another day, casting a golden glow over their garden, Sophie and Alex embraced each other, knowing that their love was a treasure—a treasure that would shine bright for eternity, a beacon of hope and inspiration for generations to come. And as they whispered promises of forever to each other, they knew that their love story was far from over—it was a story of a love that endures, a love that transcends time, and a love that would always be their greatest gift.

THIRTEEN
Embracing New Beginnings

Sophie and Alex's love story had been a journey of growth, resilience, and unwavering devotion. As they stepped into the thirteenth chapter of their lives, they found themselves at a crossroads—a moment of transition and new beginnings.

Their children, Emma and Liam, had embarked on their own paths, pursuing higher education and chasing their dreams with passion and determination. Sophie and Alex watched with pride as their children spread their wings, knowing that they had raised them to be compassionate, resilient individuals ready to face the world.

With their children's independence came a newfound sense of freedom for Sophie and Alex. They rediscovered the joy of spending time together, exploring new hobbies, and indulging in shared interests that had taken a backseat during the busy years of raising a family.

One evening, as they sat by the fireplace, Sophie turned to Alex with a smile. "Isn't it wonderful to have this time for just the two of us?" she remarked, her eyes sparkling with affection.

Alex nodded, his gaze filled with love. "It's like a new chapter in our love story," he replied, reaching for her hand. "One filled with possibilities and adventures waiting to be discovered."

They embraced this new phase of their lives with open hearts and a sense of excitement for the future. They traveled to new destinations, explored new passions, and cherished each moment spent in each other's company.

Their love had evolved over the years, deepening with every experience and challenge they had faced together. They knew that their bond was stronger than ever—a testament to the enduring power of love.

As they looked towards the horizon, Sophie and Alex knew that their love story was far from over. It was a story of resilience, growth, and the beauty of a love that continued to bloom with each passing day.

And as they welcomed new beginnings with open arms, they did so with hearts full of gratitude, love, and the unwavering certainty that their love would continue to guide them through life's ever-changing landscape—a love that stood the test of time and embraced every chapter of their journey with unwavering devotion.

FOURTEEN
Seasons of Change

Sophie and Alex had navigated through the seasons of life, from the warmth of spring to the golden hues of autumn. As they entered the fourteenth chapter of their journey, they embraced the inevitability of change—a change that brought new perspectives, renewed passion, and a deeper appreciation for the moments that mattered most.

Their home, once bustling with the laughter of children, now echoed with the tranquility of empty rooms. Emma and Liam had embarked on their own adventures, forging their paths in the world while carrying the lessons of love, resilience, and family values instilled by Sophie and Alex.

Sophie and Alex found solace in each other's company, rediscovering the intimacy and closeness that had defined the early days of their relationship. They took long walks in the park, shared quiet dinners by candlelight, and reveled in the beauty of simple moments spent together.

One evening, as they sat on their porch, watching the stars twinkle in the night sky, Sophie leaned her head against Alex's shoulder. "Do you ever miss the chaos of our younger days?" she asked softly, her voice tinged with nostalgia.

Alex wrapped his arm around her, pressing a kiss to her forehead. "Sometimes," he admitted, his gaze fixed on the stars. "But I also cherish this quiet, this closeness we share now."

Their love had evolved with time, growing deeper and more profound with each passing year. They embraced the changes that life brought, knowing that their bond was unbreakable—a source of comfort, strength, and unwavering support.

As they reflected on the chapters of their journey—the joys, the challenges, the triumphs, and the losses—they knew that every moment had shaped them into the couple they were today. They had weathered storms together, celebrated milestones, and created a life filled with love and meaning.

And as they looked towards the future, Sophie and Alex knew that their love story was far from over. It was a story of resilience, adaptation, and the enduring power of love to transcend the passage of time.

As they embraced the changing seasons of life, they did so with hearts full of gratitude, love, and the unwavering certainty that their love would continue to bloom, no matter the season or the chapter of their journey.

FIFTEEN
Reflections of a Lifetime

Sophie and Alex sat together in the quiet of their living room, surrounded by the memories of a lifetime shared. As they entered the fifteenth chapter of their journey, they reflected on the moments that had shaped their love story—the laughter, the tears, the triumphs, and the challenges that had woven the tapestry of their lives together.

Their home was filled with photographs that told the story of their love—their wedding day, family vacations, milestones celebrated, and everyday moments captured in time. Each photograph held a cherished memory, a reminder of the love that had guided them through life's ups and downs.

Sophie picked up an old photo album, flipping through the pages with a smile. "Remember when we took this trip to the mountains?" she asked, pointing to a picture of them standing on a breathtaking vista.

Alex nodded, his eyes reflecting the beauty of the memory. "It was one of the best times of our lives," he replied, his voice filled with warmth.

They reminisced about the adventures they had shared, the dreams they had pursued, and the love that had been the foundation of it all. They laughed at the silly moments and held each other close during the poignant ones, grateful for every experience that had brought them closer together.

As they sat together, surrounded by the echoes of their love story, Sophie and Alex felt a deep sense of contentment. Their journey had been a testament to the enduring power of love, a journey filled with growth, resilience, and unwavering devotion.

One evening, as they watched the sunset from their balcony, Sophie turned to Alex with tears glistening in her eyes. "Thank you for a lifetime of love," she whispered, her voice filled with emotion.

Alex held her close, pressing a kiss to her forehead. "Thank you for being my partner, my confidante, and my best friend," he replied, his heart overflowing with love.

Their love story had come full circle—a journey of a lifetime filled with love, laughter, shared dreams, and unwavering support. As they looked towards the future, Sophie and Alex knew that their love would continue to grow, evolve, and inspire—a legacy of love that would live on in the hearts of those they touched.

And as they embraced each new day together, they did so with hearts full of gratitude, love, and the unwavering certainty that their love story was a masterpiece—a reflection of a lifetime filled with love's enduring grace.

SIXTEEN
The Legacy of Love

Sophie and Alex had lived a lifetime of love—a journey marked by resilience, devotion, and the beauty of shared experiences. As they entered the sixteenth chapter of their story, they contemplated the legacy of love they had created—a legacy that would transcend time and continue to inspire generations to come.

Their children, Emma and Liam, now grown with families of their own, carried the values of love, compassion, and unity that Sophie and Alex had instilled in them. They watched with pride as their children nurtured their relationships, passed down family traditions, and embraced the enduring strength of familial bonds.

Sophie and Alex's home had become a gathering place for generations—a sanctuary where love flourished, memories were made, and stories of the past intertwined with dreams of the future. Family dinners, holiday celebrations, and quiet moments of togetherness filled their days with joy and warmth.

One day, as they sat in their garden, surrounded by laughter and love, Sophie turned to Alex with a smile. "Our legacy is love," she said, her eyes shining with pride. "A love that has shaped our family and will continue to guide us."

Alex nodded, his heart full. "Our journey has been a gift—a testament to the power of love to heal, to grow, and to unite," he replied, reaching for her hand.

Their love story had left an indelible mark on their family—a legacy of love that resonated in the hearts of their children, grandchildren, and generations to come. It was a story of resilience, passion, and the unwavering belief in the transformative power of love.

As they looked back on their journey—the highs and lows, the moments of laughter and tears, the triumphs and challenges—they knew that every chapter had led them to this moment of contentment, gratitude, and love.

And as they embraced each other, surrounded by the love of their family and the memories of a lifetime shared, Sophie and Alex knew that their legacy of love would continue to shine bright—a beacon of hope, inspiration, and the eternal beauty of love's enduring grace.

SEVENTEEN
Love's Everlasting Journey

Sophie and Alex had embarked on a journey of love that spanned a lifetime—a journey filled with moments of joy, challenges overcome, and the deepening of their bond with each passing day. As they entered the seventeenth chapter of their story, they marveled at the richness of their love's tapestry and the enduring strength it brought to their lives.

Their family had grown and flourished, with each member contributing to the legacy of love that defined their home. Emma and Liam had passed on the lessons of love, resilience, and unity to their own children, creating a ripple effect of love that touched every generation.

Sophie and Alex's home continued to be a place of warmth and togetherness, where laughter echoed through the halls and memories were cherished like precious treasures. They reveled in the company of their grandchildren, delighting in the innocence of youth and the boundless energy that filled their home.

One evening, as they sat by the fireplace, surrounded by the laughter of their grandchildren, Sophie turned to Alex with a smile. "Our love has created a legacy that will endure for generations," she remarked, her eyes shining with pride.

Alex nodded, his heart full. "It's a testament to the power of love to transcend time and leave an indelible mark on the world," he replied, his gaze filled with love for his family.

Their love story had evolved over the years, from the passion of youth to the depth of companionship that comes with a lifetime shared. They had weathered storms together, celebrated milestones, and embraced the beauty of growing old gracefully in each other's arms.

As they looked towards the future, Sophie and Alex knew that their love's journey was far from over. It was a journey of continuous growth, learning, and the unwavering belief in the transformative power of love to heal, unite, and inspire.

And as they embraced each new day with open hearts and a deep sense of gratitude, Sophie and Alex knew that their love's everlasting journey would continue to illuminate their lives, their family, and the world around them—a beacon of hope, joy, and the timeless beauty of love's enduring embrace.

EIGHTEEN
Love's Legacy in Bloom

Sophie and Alex's love had blossomed and grown, weaving a tapestry of memories, experiences, and cherished moments that spanned a lifetime. As they entered the eighteenth chapter of their story, they marveled at the legacy of love they had created—a legacy that continued to bloom and flourish in the hearts of their family and beyond.

Their home had become a sanctuary of love—a place where laughter danced on the air, where stories were shared, and where the bonds of family grew stronger with each passing day. Emma, Liam, and their families often gathered, creating new memories and honoring the traditions that had been passed down through generations.

Sophie and Alex took joy in watching their grandchildren grow, each one a testament to the enduring power of love and the values they had instilled in their family. They marveled at the way love continued to evolve, taking on new forms and shapes with each generation.

One day, as they walked hand in hand through their garden, Sophie paused to admire a blooming rose bush. "Love is like a garden," she mused, her eyes sparkling with wisdom. "It requires care, nurturing, and patience, but the rewards are beautiful beyond measure."

Alex nodded in agreement, his heart swelling with love. "Our love has blossomed into something truly extraordinary," he said, his voice filled with pride.

Their love story had been a journey of growth, transformation, and the endless capacity of the human heart to love unconditionally. They had faced challenges together, celebrated triumphs, and built a life filled with meaning and purpose.

As they looked back on their journey—the highs and lows, the laughter and tears, the moments of togetherness and solitude—they knew that their love's legacy would continue to bloom, inspiring future generations to embrace the power of love in all its forms.

And as they stood together, surrounded by the beauty of nature and the warmth of their love, Sophie and Alex knew that their story was far from over—it was a story of love's legacy in bloom, a testament to the timeless beauty of love's enduring embrace.

NINETEEN
Love's Everlasting Impact

Sophie and Alex's love had left an indelible mark on their family, their community, and the world around them. As they entered the nineteenth chapter of their story, they reflected on the impact of their love—a ripple effect that touched hearts, inspired others, and created a legacy of compassion, unity, and resilience.

Their home had become a beacon of love—a place where kindness flourished, where generosity abounded, and where the spirit of love permeated every interaction. Emma, Liam, and their families carried forward the values of love, empathy, and inclusivity, spreading love's light wherever they went.

Sophie and Alex took pride in their family's achievements, celebrating each milestone with joy and gratitude. They had built a legacy of love that extended beyond bloodlines, embracing all who crossed their path with open hearts and open arms.

One day, as they attended a family gathering, surrounded by loved ones from near and far, Sophie looked around with tears of joy in her eyes. "Our love has created a legacy that will endure for generations," she said, her voice filled with emotion.

Alex nodded, his heart swelling with love. "And it all started with us," he replied, his gaze filled with pride and gratitude.

Their love story had been a journey of discovery, growth, and the transformative power of love to change lives. They had faced adversity with courage, met challenges with resilience, and embraced each moment with a deep sense of gratitude.

As they looked towards the future, Sophie and Alex knew that their love's impact would continue to ripple outward, touching hearts and inspiring others to embrace love as the guiding force in their lives.

And as they stood together, surrounded by the love of their family and the legacy of their love, Sophie and Alex knew that their story was far from over—it was a story of love's everlasting impact, a testament to the enduring power of love to transform, heal, and unite us all.

TWENTY
Love's Eternal Promise

Sophie and Alex stood hand in hand, gazing out at the horizon as the sun dipped below the horizon, casting hues of gold and pink across the sky. As they entered the twentieth chapter of their story, they felt a profound sense of peace and fulfillment—a testament to the enduring strength of their love and the promises they had made to each other.

Their journey had been one of growth, resilience, and unwavering devotion. They had weathered life's storms together, celebrated victories, and found joy in the simple moments of togetherness.

Their home had become a sanctuary—a place where love resided in every corner, where memories were cherished, and where the legacy of their love lived on. Emma, Liam, and their families continued to thrive, carrying forward the values of love, compassion, and unity that Sophie and Alex had imparted to them.

One evening, as they sat on their porch swing, watching the stars twinkle in the night sky, Sophie turned to Alex with a smile. "Do you remember the promises we made to each other all those years ago?" she asked, her voice filled with nostalgia.

Alex nodded, his eyes reflecting the love that had endured through the years. "I promised to love you always, to stand by you through thick and thin," he replied, his voice filled with sincerity.

Sophie's heart swelled with love as she spoke her own promises. "And I promised to cherish you, to support your dreams, and to walk this journey of life with you hand in hand," she said, her eyes shining with love.

Their love story had been a testament to the power of promises kept—a journey of commitment, trust, and the unwavering belief in the enduring nature of love. They had faced challenges with grace, embraced joys with gratitude, and remained steadfast in their love for each other.

As they looked towards the future, Sophie and Alex knew that their love's promise would continue to guide them—a beacon of hope, strength, and eternal devotion.

And as they whispered words of love and gratitude to each other, under the canopy of stars and the embrace of their shared history, Sophie and Alex knew that their story was a testament to love's eternal promise—a promise of a lifetime, of a legacy that would live on in the hearts of those they loved, and of a love that would endure for all eternity.

TWENTY-ONE
Love's Endless Journey

Sophie and Alex stood side by side, gazing out at the world with hearts full of love and gratitude. As they entered the twenty-second chapter of their story, they reflected on the endless journey of love—a journey that had brought them closer together, enriched their lives, and filled their days with joy and fulfillment.

Their home had become a sanctuary—a place where love resided in every corner, where memories were cherished, and where the legacy of their love continued to bloom. Emma, Liam, and their families had grown and flourished, carrying forward the values of love, resilience, and unity that Sophie and Alex had instilled in them.

Sophie and Alex's love had transcended the boundaries of time—a timeless bond that had weathered the storms of life and emerged stronger, more vibrant, and more resilient than ever before. They had learned to navigate life's challenges with grace, to find joy in the simplest of moments, and to treasure each day as a gift.

One evening, as they sat in their garden, watching the stars twinkle in the night sky, Sophie turned to Alex with a smile. "Our love has been a journey of discovery," she remarked, her voice filled with warmth.

Alex nodded, his eyes reflecting the beauty of their shared journey. "It's a journey that has taught us the true meaning of love—to cherish each other, to support each other, and to find joy in every moment," he replied, his voice filled with love.

Their love story had been a testament to the enduring power of love—a journey of growth, transformation, and the unwavering belief in the beauty of love's endless journey. They had faced life's ups and downs with courage and resilience, knowing that their love would always be their guiding light.

As they looked towards the horizon, Sophie and Alex knew that their love's journey was far from over. It was a journey of endless possibilities, of new beginnings, and of the everlasting promise of love's embrace.

And as they embraced each other under the starlit sky, surrounded by the beauty of nature and the warmth of their love, Sophie and Alex knew that their story was a testament to love's endless journey—a journey filled with hope, joy, and the timeless beauty of love's enduring embrace.

TWENTY-TWO
Love's Endless Journey

Sophie and Alex stood side by side, gazing out at the world with hearts full of love and gratitude. As they entered the twenty-second chapter of their story, they reflected on the endless journey of love—a journey that had brought them closer together, enriched their lives, and filled their days with joy and fulfillment.

Their home had become a sanctuary—a place where love resided in every corner, where memories were cherished, and where the legacy of their love continued to bloom. Emma, Liam, and their families had grown and flourished, carrying forward the values of love, resilience, and unity that Sophie and Alex had instilled in them.

Sophie and Alex's love had transcended the boundaries of time—a timeless bond that had weathered the storms of life and emerged stronger, more vibrant, and more resilient than ever before. They had learned to navigate life's challenges with grace, to find joy in the simplest of moments, and to treasure each day as a gift.

One evening, as they sat in their garden, watching the stars twinkle in the night sky, Sophie turned to Alex with a smile. "Our love has been a journey of discovery," she remarked, her voice filled with warmth.

Alex nodded, his eyes reflecting the beauty of their shared journey. "It's a journey that has taught us the true meaning of love—to cherish each other, to support each other, and to find joy in every moment," he replied, his voice filled with love.

Their love story had been a testament to the enduring power of love—a journey of growth, transformation, and the unwavering belief in the beauty of love's endless journey. They had faced life's ups and downs with courage and resilience, knowing that their love would always be their guiding light.

As they looked towards the horizon, Sophie and Alex knew that their love's journey was far from over. It was a journey of endless possibilities, of new beginnings, and of the everlasting promise of love's embrace.

And as they embraced each other under the starlit sky, surrounded by the beauty of nature and the warmth of their love, Sophie and Alex knew that their story was a testament to love's endless journey—a journey filled with hope, joy, and the timeless beauty of love's enduring embrace.

TWENTY-THREE
Love's Boundless Horizon

Sophie and Alex stood hand in hand, their hearts intertwined like the threads of a timeless tapestry. As they entered the twenty-third chapter of their story, they marveled at the boundless horizon of love—a horizon that stretched beyond the limits of time, space, and imagination.

Their home had become a haven—a place where love flowed freely, where memories were cherished, and where the legacy of their love's journey continued to unfold. Emma, Liam, and their families had grown into pillars of strength and love, carrying forward the lessons of resilience, compassion, and unity that Sophie and Alex had imparted to them.

Sophie and Alex's love had evolved into a beacon of hope—a guiding light that illuminated their path through life's twists and turns. They had learned to embrace change, to welcome new beginnings, and to find beauty in the ebb and flow of life's journey.

One afternoon, as they sat on their favorite bench in the garden, watching the clouds drift lazily across the sky, Sophie turned to Alex with a smile. "Our love has no bounds," she remarked, her eyes sparkling with love.

Alex nodded, his gaze fixed on the horizon. "It's a love that transcends time and space—a love that knows no limits," he replied, his voice filled with wonder.

Their love story had been a testament to the infinite possibilities of love—a journey of discovery, growth, and the unbreakable bond that held them together through life's myriad adventures. They had learned to navigate challenges with grace, to find joy in the smallest of moments, and to cherish each day as a gift.

As they looked towards the horizon, Sophie and Alex knew that their love's journey was a never-ending story—a story of boundless love, endless possibilities, and the eternal beauty of love's embrace.

And as they embraced each other, their hearts beating as one, Sophie and Alex knew that their story was a testament to love's boundless horizon—a horizon that held the promise of a future filled with love, joy, and the timeless wonder of love's enduring embrace.

TWENTY-FOUR
Love's Everlasting Grace

Sophie and Alex stood beneath a canopy of stars, their love shining bright like a guiding light in the night sky. As they entered the twenty-fourth chapter of their story, they marveled at the everlasting grace of their love—a grace that had carried them through life's trials and triumphs, weaving a tapestry of love, resilience, and shared memories.

Their home had become a sanctuary—a place where love flowed freely, where laughter echoed through the halls, and where the legacy of their love's journey continued to unfold. Emma, Liam, and their families had grown and flourished, carrying forward the values of love, compassion, and unity that Sophie and Alex had instilled in them.

Sophie and Alex's love had weathered the seasons of life—a love that had deepened with time, grown stronger with adversity, and blossomed in the warmth of shared moments. They had learned to embrace the beauty of imperfection, to find strength in vulnerability, and to cherish the gift of each other's presence.

One night, as they sat by the fireplace, wrapped in the warmth of a shared blanket, Sophie turned to Alex with a smile. "Our love has been a journey of grace," she remarked, her eyes reflecting the love that filled her heart.

Alex nodded, his gaze filled with admiration. "It's a love that has taught us forgiveness, acceptance, and the true meaning of unconditional love," he replied, his voice filled with gratitude.

Their love story had been a testament to the transformative power of love—a journey of growth, healing, and the enduring bond that held them together through life's ups and downs. They had learned to let go of the past, to embrace the present moment, and to look towards the future with hope and optimism.

As they looked up at the stars, Sophie and Alex knew that their love's journey was far from over—it was a journey of endless discovery, of new beginnings, and of the everlasting grace that love bestowed upon their lives.

And as they whispered words of love and gratitude to each other, under the canopy of stars and the embrace of their shared history, Sophie and Alex knew that their story was a testament to love's everlasting grace—a grace that would continue to guide them, inspire them, and fill their lives with joy, peace, and the timeless wonder of love's enduring embrace.

TWENTY-FIVE
Love's Legacy of Hope

Sophie and Alex stood on the shores of a tranquil lake, the water shimmering in the golden light of the setting sun. As they entered the twenty-fifth chapter of their story, they reflected on the legacy of hope that their love had created—a legacy that would endure long after they were gone, inspiring future generations to embrace love, kindness, and compassion.

Their home had become a beacon of hope—a place where love's light shone brightly, where hearts were healed, and where the spirit of love's legacy lived on. Emma, Liam, and their families continued to grow and thrive, carrying forward the values of love, resilience, and generosity that Sophie and Alex had instilled in them.

Sophie and Alex's love had become a source of inspiration—a love that had overcome adversity, triumphed over challenges, and emerged stronger, more resilient, and more beautiful than ever before. They had learned to find hope in the darkest of times, to believe in the power of love to heal, and to trust in the promise of a brighter tomorrow.

One evening, as they sat on the lakeshore, watching the stars twinkle in the night sky, Sophie turned to Alex with a smile. "Our love has given us hope," she remarked, her voice filled with gratitude.

Alex nodded, his eyes reflecting the light of the stars. "It's a love that has taught us to see the beauty in every moment, to cherish the gift of life, and to believe in the limitless possibilities of tomorrow," he replied, his voice filled with hope.

Their love story had been a testament to the resilience of the human spirit—a journey of courage, faith, and the unwavering belief in the power of love to transform lives. They had faced challenges with grace, embraced joy with gratitude, and found strength in each other's embrace.

As they looked out at the tranquil lake, Sophie and Alex knew that their love's legacy of hope would continue to inspire, uplift, and empower others to believe in the power of love to create a better world.

And as they held each other close, their hearts beating in rhythm with the beauty of nature and the promise of a new day, Sophie and Alex knew that their story was a testament to love's enduring legacy of hope—a legacy that would live on in the hearts of those they touched, guiding them towards a future filled with love, joy, and endless possibilities.

TWENTY-SIX
Love's Infinite Horizon

Sophie and Alex stood at the edge of a cliff, overlooking a vast and endless horizon. As they entered the twenty-sixth chapter of their story, they marveled at the infinite possibilities that love had brought into their lives—a journey of discovery, growth, and the boundless beauty of love's embrace.

Their home had become a sanctuary of love—a place where hearts were filled with joy, where laughter echoed through the halls, and where the legacy of their love's journey continued to unfold. Emma, Liam, and their families had grown and flourished, carrying forward the values of love, compassion, and unity that Sophie and Alex had passed down to them.

Sophie and Alex's love had expanded beyond the confines of their home—a love that had touched lives, inspired hearts, and left a lasting impact on the world around them. They had learned to embrace diversity, to celebrate differences, and to find beauty in the interconnectedness of all living beings.

One day, as they walked along the cliff's edge, feeling the gentle breeze on their faces, Sophie turned to Alex with a smile. "Our love has no limits," she remarked, her eyes sparkling with wonder.

Alex nodded, his gaze fixed on the horizon. "It's a love that transcends boundaries, bridges divides, and unites us all in a shared journey of love and compassion," he replied, his voice filled with awe.

Their love story had been a testament to the transformative power of love—a journey of exploration, discovery, and the boundless potential of the human heart to love unconditionally. They had faced challenges with courage, embraced diversity with open minds, and found beauty in the tapestry of life's experiences.

As they looked out at the endless horizon, Sophie and Alex knew that their love's journey was far from over—it was a journey of endless discovery, of new beginnings, and of the infinite possibilities that love held for their future.

And as they stood together, their hearts intertwined and their souls connected in love's embrace, Sophie and Alex knew that their story was a testament to love's infinite horizon—a horizon that stretched beyond the limits of imagination, filled with promise, hope, and the eternal wonder of love's enduring embrace.

TWENTY-SEVEN
Love's Unbroken Circle

Sophie and Alex stood beneath a canopy of trees, their hands clasped together in a timeless embrace. As they entered the twenty-seventh chapter of their story, they marveled at the unbroken circle of love that had guided them through life's journeys—a circle of love that had no beginning and no end, but simply existed in the eternal now.

Their home had become a haven of love—a place where hearts were nourished, where dreams took flight, and where the legacy of their love's journey continued to unfold. Emma, Liam, and their families had grown and thrived, carrying forward the values of love, kindness, and resilience that Sophie and Alex had instilled in them.

Sophie and Alex's love had transcended time—a love that had spanned decades, weathered storms, and grown stronger with each passing day. They had learned to embrace the beauty of impermanence, to cherish each moment as a gift, and to find joy in the journey itself.

One evening, as they sat by a crackling fire, watching the flames dance in the darkness, Sophie turned to Alex with a smile. "Our love is like a circle," she remarked, her voice filled with warmth.

Alex nodded, his eyes reflecting the light of the fire. "It's a love that has no beginning and no end—a love that continues to evolve, to grow, and to inspire us every day," he replied, his voice filled with gratitude.

Their love story had been a testament to the cyclical nature of life—a journey of beginnings and endings, of growth and transformation, and of the eternal cycle of love's embrace. They had faced challenges with resilience, celebrated victories with humility, and found solace in the rhythm of life's ebb and flow.

As they looked up at the starry sky, Sophie and Alex knew that their love's circle was unbroken—it was a circle of love, of hope, and of the eternal bond that held them together through all of life's adventures.

And as they held each other close, their hearts beating in sync with the universe, Sophie and Alex knew that their story was a testament to love's unbroken circle—a circle that would continue to guide them, inspire them, and fill their lives with the infinite beauty of love's enduring embrace.

TWENTY-EIGHT
Love's Resilient Spirit

Sophie and Alex walked hand in hand through a field of wildflowers, their hearts filled with the resilient spirit of love that had carried them through life's challenges. As they entered the twenty-eighth chapter of their story, they marveled at the strength, courage, and unwavering determination that their love had inspired in them.

Their home had become a sanctuary of resilience—a place where hearts healed, where dreams flourished, and where the legacy of their love's journey continued to unfold. Emma, Liam, and their families had grown into resilient individuals, carrying forward the lessons of perseverance, faith, and optimism that Sophie and Alex had imparted to them.

Sophie and Alex's love had weathered storms—a love that had stood strong in the face of adversity, grown deeper through trials, and blossomed in the light of shared victories. They had learned to embrace change with open hearts, to find strength in vulnerability, and to trust in the power of love to overcome all obstacles.

One afternoon, as they sat under a tree, the sunlight filtering through the leaves, Sophie turned to Alex with a smile. "Our love is resilient," she remarked, her eyes reflecting the strength that their love had instilled in them.

Alex nodded, his gaze filled with determination. "It's a love that has taught us to persevere, to never give up, and to believe in the resilience of the human spirit," he replied, his voice filled with conviction.

Their love story had been a testament to the indomitable spirit of love—a journey of resilience, growth, and the unwavering belief in the power of love to overcome all challenges. They had faced adversity with grace, embraced change with courage, and emerged stronger, wiser, and more resilient than ever before.

As they looked out at the field of wildflowers, swaying gently in the breeze, Sophie and Alex knew that their love's resilience would continue to guide them—a beacon of hope, strength, and unwavering faith in the face of life's uncertainties.

And as they embraced each other, their hearts beating in rhythm with the resilient spirit of love, Sophie and Alex knew that their story was a testament to love's enduring resilience—a resilience that would continue to inspire, uplift, and empower others to embrace life's challenges with courage, grace, and the unwavering belief in the power of love to conquer all.

TWENTY-NINE
Love's Timeless Journey

Sophie and Alex stood at a crossroads, their hearts filled with gratitude for the timeless journey of love that had brought them to this moment. As they entered the twenty-ninth chapter of their story, they marveled at the depth, richness, and enduring beauty of their love—a love that had stood the test of time and continued to evolve with each passing day.

Their home had become a tapestry of memories—a place where love's journey was woven into every thread, where stories were told, and where the legacy of their love's journey continued to unfold. Emma, Liam, and their families had grown and flourished, carrying forward the values of love, compassion, and unity that Sophie and Alex had instilled in them.

Sophie and Alex's love had transcended the boundaries of ordinary life—a love that had grown deeper with each shared experience, blossomed in moments of joy, and found strength in moments of adversity. They had learned to navigate life's twists and turns with grace, to cherish the beauty of the present moment, and to embrace the uncertainty of the future with open hearts.

One evening, as they sat on their porch swing, watching the sun set on another day, Sophie turned to Alex with a smile. "Our love is a timeless journey," she remarked, her voice filled with wonder.

Alex nodded, his eyes reflecting the beauty of their shared journey. "It's a journey that has enriched our lives, shaped our destinies, and brought us closer together with each passing day," he replied, his voice filled with love.

Their love story had been a testament to the enduring nature of love—a journey of discovery, growth, and the timeless beauty of love's embrace. They had learned to savor each moment, to celebrate each milestone, and to find joy in the journey itself.

As they looked out at the horizon, bathed in the warm glow of the setting sun, Sophie and Alex knew that their love's journey was far from over—it was a journey of endless discovery, of new beginnings, and of the timeless wonder of love's enduring embrace.

And as they whispered words of love and gratitude to each other, under the vast expanse of the starlit sky, Sophie and Alex knew that their story was a testament to love's timeless journey—a journey filled with hope, joy, and the eternal beauty of love's enduring embrace.

THIRTY
Love's Everlasting Promise

Sophie and Alex stood hand in hand, their hearts intertwined in the warmth of a love that knew no bounds. As they entered the thirtieth chapter of their story, they reflected on the everlasting promise of love—a promise that had guided them through life's highs and lows, and had remained steadfast through the passage of time.

Their home had become a sanctuary of love—a place where memories were cherished, where laughter echoed through the halls, and where the legacy of their love's journey continued to unfold. Emma, Liam, and their families had grown into individuals of integrity, compassion, and kindness, carrying forward the values of love that Sophie and Alex had nurtured in them.

Sophie and Alex's love had transcended the ordinary—a love that had blossomed in the tender moments, grown stronger in the face of challenges, and flourished in the shared dreams they had built together. They had learned to embrace the seasons of life with grace, to find solace in each other's presence, and to trust in the power of their love to light their way forward.

One night, as they sat by the fireplace, the flames casting a warm glow on their faces, Sophie turned to Alex with a smile. "Our love is an everlasting promise," she remarked, her voice filled with love.

Alex nodded, his eyes reflecting the depth of their bond. "It's a promise that we made to each other—to be there through thick and thin, to support and cherish each other, and to journey through life hand in hand," he replied, his voice filled with devotion.

Their love story had been a testament to the enduring commitment of love—a journey of dedication, loyalty, and the unbreakable promise that they had made to each other. They had faced challenges together, celebrated victories together, and had grown together in love and understanding.

As they looked out at the starry sky, a blanket of twinkling lights above them, Sophie and Alex knew that their love's promise was unyielding—it was a promise of a future filled with love, joy, and the eternal bond that held them together.

And as they leaned into each other's embrace, their hearts beating in sync with the rhythm of their love, Sophie and Alex knew that their story was a testament to love's everlasting promise—a promise that would continue to guide them, inspire them, and fill their lives with the infinite beauty of love's enduring embrace.

THIRTY-ONE
Love's Eternal Legacy

Sophie and Alex stood beneath the starlit sky, surrounded by the echoes of their shared journey and the whispers of love's eternal legacy. As they entered the thirty-first chapter of their story, they reflected on the legacy of love that they had built—a legacy that would continue to inspire, uplift, and nurture hearts for generations to come.

Their home had become a beacon of love—a place where hearts found solace, where dreams took flight, and where the legacy of their love's journey continued to unfold. Emma, Liam, and their families had grown into compassionate individuals, carrying forward the values of love, resilience, and unity that Sophie and Alex had instilled in them.

Sophie and Alex's love had left an indelible mark on the world—a love that had touched lives, transformed hearts, and created a ripple effect of kindness and compassion. They had learned to lead by example, to live with purpose and intention, and to leave behind a legacy of love that would endure beyond their time.

One evening, as they sat on their porch swing, the moon casting a gentle glow around them, Sophie turned to Alex with a smile. "Our love's legacy is eternal," she remarked, her voice filled with gratitude.

Alex nodded, his eyes reflecting the depth of their impact. "It's a legacy of love that will continue to inspire, uplift, and unite hearts long after we're gone," he replied, his voice filled with pride.

Their love story had been a testament to the transformative power of love—a journey of growth, discovery, and the everlasting impact of love's embrace. They had learned to live with purpose, to lead with love, and to leave behind a legacy that would stand as a testament to their enduring bond.

As they looked out at the starry sky, a canvas of infinite possibilities above them, Sophie and Alex knew that their love's legacy would live on—it was a legacy of love, of hope, and of the eternal beauty of love's enduring embrace.

And as they held each other close, their hearts beating in rhythm with the universe, Sophie and Alex knew that their story was a testament to love's eternal legacy—a legacy that would continue to shine brightly, guiding hearts towards a future filled with love, compassion, and the timeless wonder of love's enduring embrace.

THIRTY-TWO
Love's Unending Journey

Sophie and Alex stood hand in hand, gazing into each other's eyes with a love that had stood the test of time. As they entered the thirty-second chapter of their story, they marveled at the unending journey of love—a journey filled with laughter, tears, triumphs, and challenges, yet always guided by the unwavering bond they shared.

Their home had become a sanctuary of love—a place where hearts found refuge, where memories were treasured, and where the legacy of their love's journey continued to unfold. Emma, Liam, and their families had grown into beacons of love and compassion, carrying forward the values of kindness, resilience, and unity that Sophie and Alex had passed down to them.

Sophie and Alex's love had transcended the ordinary—a love that had deepened with every passing day, grown more profound with every shared experience, and flourished in the warmth of their mutual understanding and support. They had learned to navigate life's twists and turns with grace, to cherish each other's presence, and to celebrate the gift of their love.

One night, as they sat by the window, watching the stars twinkle in the vast expanse of the night sky, Sophie turned to Alex with a smile. "Our love's journey is unending," she remarked, her voice filled with joy.

Alex nodded, his eyes reflecting the depth of their connection. "It's a journey of discovery, growth, and endless possibilities—a journey that we embark on together, hand in hand," he replied, his voice filled with love.

Their love story had been a testament to the resilience of the human heart—a journey of faith, hope, and the unyielding belief in the power of love to conquer all. They had faced challenges with courage, embraced joys with gratitude, and had grown together in love, understanding, and mutual respect.

As they looked out at the night sky, a tapestry of stars above them, Sophie and Alex knew that their love's journey would continue—it was a journey of unending discovery, of new beginnings, and of the infinite beauty of love's enduring embrace.

And as they embraced each other, their hearts beating in sync with the rhythm of the universe, Sophie and Alex knew that their story was a testament to love's unending journey—a journey filled with love, joy, and the timeless wonder of love's enduring embrace.

THIRTY-THREE
Love's Boundless Horizon

Sophie and Alex stood on a hilltop, overlooking a breathtaking vista that stretched as far as the eye could see. As they entered the thirty-third chapter of their story, they marveled at the boundless horizon of possibilities that their love had opened up—a horizon filled with dreams, aspirations, and the endless potential of their shared journey.

Their home had become a haven of love—a place where hearts were nurtured, where dreams took flight, and where the legacy of their love's journey continued to unfold. Emma, Liam, and their families had grown into compassionate and resilient individuals, carrying forward the values of love, kindness, and perseverance that Sophie and Alex had instilled in them.

Sophie and Alex's love had transcended limitations—a love that had defied odds, broken barriers, and soared to new heights of understanding and connection. They had learned to embrace change with open hearts, to find beauty in life's uncertainties, and to trust in the power of their love to guide them through every challenge.

One evening, as they sat beneath the stars, their silhouettes outlined against the night sky, Sophie turned to Alex with a smile. "Our love has shown us a boundless horizon," she remarked, her voice filled with wonder.

Alex nodded, his eyes reflecting the vastness of their love. "It's a horizon of endless possibilities, of dreams yet to be realized, and of adventures waiting to unfold," he replied, his voice filled with excitement.

Their love story had been a testament to the transformative nature of love—a journey of growth, discovery, and the boundless potential of the human heart to love unconditionally. They had faced challenges with resilience, celebrated triumphs with humility, and had grown together in love, faith, and mutual respect.

As they looked out at the expansive horizon, a canvas of infinite possibilities before them, Sophie and Alex knew that their love's journey was far from over—it was a journey of boundless exploration, of new horizons, and of the limitless wonder of love's enduring embrace.

And as they embraced each other, their hearts beating in rhythm with the universe, Sophie and Alex knew that their story was a testament to love's boundless horizon—a horizon that would continue to inspire, uplift, and guide them towards a future filled with love, joy, and endless possibilities.

THIRTY-FOUR
Love's Everlasting Tapestry

Sophie and Alex walked hand in hand through a garden blooming with vibrant flowers, each blossom a symbol of the colors and emotions woven into the tapestry of their love. As they entered the thirty-fourth chapter of their story, they marveled at the everlasting tapestry of love that had been crafted from moments of joy, sorrow, laughter, and tears.

Their home had become a sanctuary of love—a place where hearts found solace, where memories were cherished, and where the legacy of their love's journey continued to unfold. Emma, Liam, and their families had grown into compassionate and resilient individuals, carrying forward the values of love, empathy, and perseverance that Sophie and Alex had instilled in them.

Sophie and Alex's love had woven threads of connection—a love that had intertwined their lives in a beautiful tapestry of shared experiences, lessons learned, and growth achieved. They had learned to appreciate the beauty of each thread, to embrace imperfections as part of the whole, and to find harmony in the diversity of their love's colors.

One afternoon, as they sat in their garden, surrounded by the fragrance of blooming flowers, Sophie turned to Alex with a smile. "Our love is like an everlasting tapestry," she remarked, her eyes sparkling with affection.

Alex nodded, his gaze sweeping over the garden. "It's a tapestry woven with moments of love, kindness, and understanding—a tapestry that tells the story of our journey together," he replied, his voice filled with love.

Their love story had been a testament to the intricate beauty of love—a journey of connection, growth, and the timeless elegance of love's embrace. They had faced challenges with resilience, celebrated victories with humility, and had grown together as individuals and as partners in love.

As they looked at the garden, each flower a testament to a moment shared, Sophie and Alex knew that their love's tapestry would continue to evolve—it was a tapestry of endless possibilities, of new chapters waiting to be written, and of the eternal beauty of love's enduring embrace.

And as they embraced each other, their hearts beating in sync with the rhythm of nature, Sophie and Alex knew that their story was a testament to love's everlasting tapestry—a tapestry that would continue to unfold, revealing new patterns of love, joy, and endless discoveries in the chapters yet to come.

THIRTY-FIVE
Love's Infinite Symphony

Sophie and Alex stood by a tranquil lake, the water reflecting the golden hues of the setting sun, creating a serene backdrop for the next chapter of their journey. As they entered the thirty-fifth chapter of their story, they marveled at the infinite symphony of love that had played out in their lives—a symphony filled with melodies of joy, harmony, and the timeless rhythm of their hearts beating as one.

Their home had become a symphony hall of love—a place where hearts resonated with the music of shared experiences, where dreams harmonized with reality, and where the legacy of their love's journey continued to unfold. Emma, Liam, and their families had grown into compassionate and empathetic individuals, carrying forward the melodies of love, kindness, and unity that Sophie and Alex had composed for them.

Sophie and Alex's love had conducted symphonies of connection—a love that had orchestrated moments of togetherness, unity, and understanding. They had learned to listen to each other's hearts, to dance to the rhythm of life's melodies, and to find beauty in the harmonies that emerged from their shared journey.

One evening, as they sat by the lake, the gentle lapping of water against the shore creating a soothing melody, Sophie turned to Alex with a smile. "Our love is like an infinite symphony," she remarked, her voice filled with appreciation.

Alex nodded, his eyes reflecting the beauty of their shared music. "It's a symphony that continues to evolve, to crescendo with each passing moment, and to fill our lives with the eternal melodies of love," he replied, his voice filled with love.

Their love story had been a testament to the transformative power of music—a journey of harmony, rhythm, and the timeless beauty of love's embrace. They had faced life's compositions with grace, celebrated the symphonies of joy, and had grown together as composers of their love's melodies.

As they listened to the symphony of nature around them, the rustling of leaves, the chirping of birds, Sophie and Alex knew that their love's symphony would continue—it was a symphony of endless variations, of new harmonies waiting to be discovered, and of the infinite beauty of love's enduring embrace.

And as they embraced each other, their hearts beating in sync with the universe's symphony, Sophie and Alex knew that their story was a testament to love's infinite symphony—a symphony that would continue to play on, resonating with the hearts of all who listened, and filling their lives with the timeless magic of love's eternal melody.

THIRTY-SIX
Love's Evergreen Legacy

Sophie and Alex walked through a forest of evergreen trees, their branches reaching towards the sky in a timeless dance of resilience and strength. As they entered the thirty-sixth chapter of their story, they marveled at the evergreen legacy of love that had taken root in their hearts—a legacy that would continue to flourish and inspire for generations to come.

Their home had become a sanctuary of love—a place where hearts found solace, where dreams took root, and where the legacy of their love's journey continued to unfold. Emma, Liam, and their families had grown into compassionate and courageous individuals, carrying forward the values of love, perseverance, and unity that Sophie and Alex had planted in them.

Sophie and Alex's love had grown like the evergreens—a love that had weathered storms, stood tall in adversity, and remained vibrant and resilient through life's changing seasons. They had learned to find strength in each other, to draw nourishment from their shared roots, and to embrace the beauty of growth and renewal.

One morning, as they sat under the shade of an evergreen, the sunlight filtering through the branches, Sophie turned to Alex with a smile. "Our love is like these evergreen trees," she remarked, her voice filled with reverence.

Alex nodded, his eyes tracing the patterns of sunlight on the forest floor. "It's a love that remains green and vibrant, regardless of the seasons that pass—a love that continues to bloom and flourish with each passing day," he replied, his voice filled with gratitude.

Their love story had been a testament to the enduring nature of love—a journey of resilience, growth, and the everlasting legacy of love's embrace. They had faced challenges with courage, celebrated victories with humility, and had grown together in love, wisdom, and mutual respect.

As they looked at the forest around them, each tree a symbol of strength and endurance, Sophie and Alex knew that their love's legacy would continue—it was a legacy of evergreen love, of renewal, and of the timeless beauty of love's enduring embrace.

And as they embraced each other, their hearts beating in rhythm with the pulse of nature, Sophie and Alex knew that their story was a testament to love's evergreen legacy—a legacy that would continue to inspire, nurture, and flourish, like the eternal love that bound their hearts together.

THIRTY-SEVEN
Love's Endless Journey

Sophie and Alex stood at a crossroads, their eyes filled with the reflections of the countless moments that had shaped their love. As they entered the thirty-seventh chapter of their story, they embraced the realization that their love was not just a destination but an endless journey—a journey of growth, discovery, and the boundless depths of their hearts intertwined.

Their home had become a haven of love—a place where hearts found refuge, where dreams were nurtured, and where the legacy of their love's journey continued to unfold. Emma, Liam, and their families had grown into beacons of love and compassion, carrying forward the values of kindness, empathy, and resilience that Sophie and Alex had imparted to them.

Sophie and Alex's love had traversed paths unknown—a love that had ventured into the depths of their souls, explored the heights of their dreams, and embraced the mysteries of life's unfolding journey. They had learned to cherish each moment, to savor each experience, and to find beauty in the ebb and flow of their shared existence.

One evening, as they sat under a canopy of stars, the universe unfolding its secrets above them, Sophie turned to Alex with a smile. "Our love's journey is endless," she remarked, her voice filled with wonder.

Alex nodded, his gaze meeting hers with a depth of understanding. "It's a journey of discovery, of endless possibilities, and of the eternal bond that binds our hearts together," he replied, his voice filled with love.

Their love story had been a testament to the vastness of love—an exploration of the human spirit, of resilience, and of the timeless connection that transcended time and space. They had faced challenges with courage, embraced joys with gratitude, and had grown together as partners in the grand adventure of life.

As they looked up at the stars, a tapestry of light shimmering in the vast expanse of the night sky, Sophie and Alex knew that their love's journey would continue—it was a journey of endless exploration, of new beginnings, and of the infinite beauty of love's enduring embrace.

And as they held each other close, their hearts beating in sync with the rhythm of the universe, Sophie and Alex knew that their story was a testament to love's endless journey—a journey that would continue to unfold, revealing new chapters, new discoveries, and new depths of love's boundless essence.

THIRTY-EIGHT
Love's Unbreakable Bond

Sophie and Alex sat by a roaring fireplace, the crackling of the flames a soothing melody that accompanied the next chapter of their journey together. As they entered the thirty-eighth chapter of their story, they reflected on the unbreakable bond that had held their hearts together through every twist and turn of life's intricate dance.

Their home had become a sanctuary of love—a place where hearts found solace, where dreams took flight, and where the legacy of their love's journey continued to weave its magic. Emma, Liam, and their families had grown into pillars of strength and compassion, carrying forward the torch of love, resilience, and unity that Sophie and Alex had ignited in them.

Sophie and Alex's love had forged an unbreakable bond—a bond that had weathered storms, stood strong in adversity, and remained steadfast through the passage of time. They had learned to lean on each other in moments of doubt, to lift each other up in times of need, and to trust in the power of their bond to guide them through life's challenges.

One night, as they sat by the fireplace, the warmth of the flames enveloping them in a cocoon of comfort, Sophie turned to Alex with a smile. "Our love's bond is unbreakable," she remarked, her voice filled with certainty.

Alex nodded, his eyes reflecting the depth of their connection. "It's a bond forged in the fires of life's trials, tempered by love, and strengthened by our unwavering commitment to each other," he replied, his voice filled with love.

Their love story had been a testament to the resilience of love—an exploration of trust, loyalty, and the enduring power of a bond that transcended the ordinary. They had faced challenges head-on, embraced victories with humility, and had grown together as partners in love and in life.

As they sat in the glow of the fire, the flames casting dancing shadows on the walls, Sophie and Alex knew that their love's bond was unbreakable—it was a bond of shared experiences, of mutual respect, and of the eternal promise to stand by each other's side, no matter what life may bring.

And as they embraced, their hearts beating in sync with the rhythm of their love, Sophie and Alex knew that their story was a testament to love's unbreakable bond—a bond that would continue to hold them together, to guide them through life's journeys, and to illuminate their path with the timeless beauty of love's enduring embrace.

THIRTY-NINE
Love's Radiant Legacy

Sophie and Alex stood under a canopy of cherry blossoms, the delicate petals fluttering in the breeze like whispers of love that echoed the next chapter of their journey. As they entered the thirty-ninth chapter of their story, they marveled at the radiant legacy of love they had created—a legacy that would continue to bloom and inspire for generations to come.

Their home had become a garden of love—a place where hearts blossomed, where dreams took root, and where the legacy of their love's journey continued to unfold. Emma, Liam, and their families had grown into beacons of light and kindness, carrying forward the values of love, compassion, and resilience that Sophie and Alex had sown in them.

Sophie and Alex's love had bloomed like the cherry blossoms—a love that had flourished in the sunshine of happiness, weathered the storms of challenges, and remained resilient through the changing seasons of life. They had learned to appreciate the beauty of each moment, to find joy in simple pleasures, and to cherish the memories they created together.

One spring day, as they walked hand in hand through the blooming cherry blossom trees, Sophie turned to Alex with a smile. "Our love's legacy is radiant," she remarked, her voice filled with admiration.

Alex nodded, his eyes sparkling with love. "It's a legacy of beauty, of growth, and of the everlasting impact of love's embrace on our hearts and those around us," he replied, his voice filled with gratitude.

Their love story had been a testament to the transformative power of love—a journey of growth, discovery, and the timeless beauty of love's enduring embrace. They had faced challenges with courage, celebrated joys with gratitude, and had grown together in love, wisdom, and compassion.

As they walked among the cherry blossoms, each flower a symbol of their love's legacy, Sophie and Alex knew that their journey was far from over—it was a journey of endless growth, of new beginnings, and of the infinite radiance of love's enduring embrace.

And as they embraced each other beneath the blooming trees, their hearts beating in sync with the rhythm of nature, Sophie and Alex knew that their story was a testament to love's radiant legacy—a legacy that would continue to inspire, uplift, and bloom with the timeless beauty of love's enduring embrace.

FORTY
Love's Eternal Promise

Sophie and Alex stood at the edge of a cliff, overlooking a vast ocean that stretched to the horizon, symbolizing the endless possibilities that lay ahead in the final chapter of their story. As they entered this milestone, the fortieth chapter, they reflected on the eternal promise of their love—a promise that transcended time, space, and all obstacles.

Their home had become a sanctuary of love—a place where hearts found peace, where dreams took flight, and where the legacy of their love's journey continued to inspire. Emma, Liam, and their families had grown into pillars of strength and compassion, carrying forward the values of love, resilience, and unity that Sophie and Alex had instilled in them.

Sophie and Alex's love had stood the test of time—a love that had endured through life's trials, remained steadfast in moments of doubt, and grown stronger with each passing day. They had learned the true meaning of commitment, of devotion, and of the unbreakable bond that bound their hearts together.

One evening, as they watched the sun set over the ocean, painting the sky in hues of orange and pink, Sophie turned to Alex with a smile. "Our love's promise is eternal," she remarked, her voice filled with certainty.

Alex nodded, his eyes reflecting the beauty of the sunset. "It's a promise of forever, of unwavering support, and of the boundless love that will guide us through all of life's adventures," he replied, his voice filled with love.

Their love story had been a testament to the enduring nature of love—a journey of growth, discovery, and the timeless essence of love's embrace. They had faced challenges with courage, celebrated victories with humility, and had grown together as partners in love and in life.

As they stood at the cliff's edge, the vastness of the ocean before them, Sophie and Alex knew that their love's promise was eternal—it was a promise of endless love, of shared dreams, and of the infinite possibilities that awaited them on their journey together.

And as they embraced, their hearts beating in sync with the rhythm of the waves below, Sophie and Alex knew that their story was a testament to love's eternal promise—a promise that would continue to guide them, inspire them, and fill their lives with the timeless beauty of love's enduring embrace.

FORTY-ONE
Epilogue: Love's Timeless Legacy

Sophie and Alex sat on their favorite bench in the park, watching the sunset paint the sky in a symphony of colors. As they reflected on their journey together, they marveled at the legacy of love they had created—a legacy that would live on in the hearts of all who knew them.

Their home had become a beacon of love—a place where memories were cherished, where laughter echoed through the halls, and where the legacy of their love's journey continued to inspire. Emma, Liam, and their families had grown into compassionate and resilient individuals, carrying forward the values of love, kindness, and unity that Sophie and Alex had instilled in them.

Sophie and Alex's love had touched countless lives—a love that had radiated warmth, brought hope, and shown the world the true meaning of devotion. They had weathered life's storms together, celebrated life's joys together, and had grown old together, hand in hand, their love only deepening with each passing year.

One evening, as they watched the stars twinkle in the night sky, Sophie turned to Alex with a smile. "Our love's legacy is timeless," she remarked, her voice filled with gratitude.

Alex nodded, his eyes reflecting the love that had defined their lives. "It's a legacy of love, of laughter, and of the beautiful moments we've shared together," he replied, his voice filled with love.

Their love story had been a testament to the power of love—a journey of growth, discovery, and the enduring beauty of love's embrace. They had faced life's challenges with grace, celebrated life's blessings with humility, and had built a life filled with love, joy, and cherished memories.

As they sat together, their hearts beating in rhythm with the universe, Sophie and Alex knew that their story was complete—a story of love's enduring legacy, of a bond that transcended time and space, and of a love that would live on forever in the hearts of those who had been touched by it.

And as they leaned into each other, their hands entwined, Sophie and Alex knew that their love was eternal—a love that would continue to inspire, uplift, and shine as a beacon of hope and happiness for all eternity.

Closing Words

End Matter

Congratulations on reaching the end of "First Love in Paris"! We hope this journey through the romantic streets of Paris has left you with a heart full of joy and a smile on your face.

As you close this book, remember that love is a timeless adventure, filled with unexpected twists, delightful moments, and endless possibilities. May the love story of Marie and Pierre continue to inspire you to cherish the magic of first love and to embrace every moment with an open heart.

Thank you for joining us on this enchanting journey. We invite you to stay connected and discover more captivating tales in the world of literature.

With warm regards and best wishes,
Mikey Katodiya

Did you love *First Love in Paris*? Then you should read *Yesterday's Love Story*[1] by Mikey Katodiya!

[2]

As I sit down to pen the story of my life, I find myself traversing through a tapestry of emotions, memories, and experiences that have defined my journey. It's a story of love, friendship, loss, and the resilience that has shaped my existence. My life's narrative begins in the hallowed halls of school, where I was just another ordinary student, navigating the complexities of growing up. Little did I know that my life would take an extraordinary turn when I crossed paths with Riya, a girl whose presence would transform my world. The heart of this tale revolves around our profound and heartfelt relationship. From the early days of youthful innocence to the challenges of young love, Riya and I experienced the full spectrum of emotions together. Our journey

1. https://books2read.com/u/3kO6OR

2. https://books2read.com/u/3kO6OR

was filled with moments of joy, heartache, and personal growth, leaving an indelible mark on our souls. Throughout this narrative, you'll discover the significance of friendship, the unwavering support of friends like Janamay and Jatin, and the harsh realities of dealing with toxic relationships. These elements add depth and authenticity to my story, showcasing the importance of genuine connections in life. However, life is not without its trials and tribulations. The story takes an unexpected turn when Riya faces a traumatic brain injury. This unforeseen circumstance forces me to confront the fragility of life and the depth of our love. Riya's heartfelt letter, left for me after her passing, is a testament to the enduring power of love and its ability to heal even the deepest wounds. " Yesterday's Love Story" is more than just a recounting of events; it's an exploration of the human spirit's capacity to endure, adapt, and find hope in the face of adversity. Through the highs and lows, this story underscores the significance of cherishing every moment and finding the strength to embrace life's uncertainties. In the end, " Yesterday's Love Story" is a poignant reminder that life's greatest lessons often emerge from the most challenging chapters. It's a story of love and loss, resilience, and the unwavering bonds that tie us together, even when faced with the harshest of realities.

About the Author

Meet, who often goes by the pen name "Mikey," is a passionate writer who believes in the power of storytelling to inspire and heal. Writing has been his creative outlet, allowing him to explore complex emotions and share them with others. 'Yesterday's Love Story' is his debut work, born frompersonal experiences and a desire to connect with readers on a deeply emotional level. Meet hopes his words, written under the pen nameMikey, will resonate with those seeking solace and strength in the face of adversity.

Read more at https://www.instagram.com/bigpicstory.